Dear Parent:
Your child's love of reading starts here!

Every child learns to read in a different way and at his or her own speed. Some go back and forth between reading levels and read favorite books again and again. Others read through each level in order. You can help your young reader improve and become more confident by encouraging his or her own interests and abilities. From books your child reads with you to the first books he or she reads alone, there are I Can Read Books for every stage of reading:

SHARED READING
Basic language, word repetition, and whimsical illustrations, ideal for sharing with your emergent reader

BEGINNING READING
Short sentences, familiar words, and simple concepts for children eager to read on their own

READING WITH HELP
Engaging stories, longer sentences, and language play for developing readers

READING ALONE
Complex plots, challenging vocabulary, and high-interest topics for the independent reader

ADVANCED READING
Short paragraphs, chapters, and exciting themes for the perfect bridge to chapter books

I Can Read Books have introduced children to the joy of reading since 1957. Featuring award-winning authors and illustrators and a fabulous cast of beloved characters, I Can Read Books set the standard for beginning readers.

A lifetime of discovery begins with the magical words **"I Can Read!"**

Visit www.icanread.com for information on enriching your child's reading experience.

Earth Day Fun

by Jennifer Frantz

HARPER

An Imprint of HarperCollinsPublishers

"Guess what?" said Sid.
"Dad and I are
doing something extra cool
after school today."

"We're planting a tree!

And not just any tree.

It is a brand-new baby tree.

Dad says trees are good

for our planet, Earth.

Plus, we get to play in the dirt!"

"Mom doesn't always like it when I play in the dirt. It gets on my clothes and toys and sometimes on the walls."

"But dirt can't help

getting things dirty.

What is in dirt, anyway?"

"Good morning, Sid," said Mom.

"Morning!" said Sid.

"Mom, I was just wondering,

why don't you like dirt?"

"I like dirt fine,

when it's outside," said Mom.

"Did you know

that there are many kinds of dirt?"

"There is potting soil," said Mom.

"There is the dirt in our yard.

And there is desert dirt,

which is mostly made of sand."

"Dad bought potting soil

to use when you plant your tree.

It's dirt for planting things."

"Cool!" said Sid.

"I'll dig into this more at school."

At school, Sid found his friends.

"Hey, guys!" said Sid.

"What do you think is in dirt?"

"I know!" said Gabriela.

"Dirt has stuff in it

that is good for plants and trees."

"Dirt has worms in it!" said May.

"I saw one and I named it Mortimer."

"I know all about dirt,"

said Gerald.

"I play in dirt piles a lot.

Dirt is full of tiny rocks."

"Good answers!" said Sid.

In class, Sid told Teacher Susie
about the tree he would plant.
"My dad says it's Earth Day,"
he said.

"It sure is!" Teacher Susie said.

"And we can make

every day Earth Day

by taking care of our planet."

"We need to take care of the trees,"
said Gerald.

"And the animals," said Gabriela.

"And the oceans," said May.

"Right on!" said Teacher Susie.

"We need to keep dirt clean, too.

Dirt, or soil, is very important.

Let's find out why

in the Super Fab Lab!"

"What makes soil so important?"
asked Teacher Susie.

"Trees grow in soil," said Sid.

"Vegetables do, too," said May.

"Like spinach. Yuck," said Gerald.

"Very good, Dirt Detectives!

Now, let's find out what's in soil."

Dirt Detective Sid and his friends

took a close look at their soil.

"The soil is all different colors,"
said Gabriela.

"But I found a plastic straw, too,"
she said.

"That doesn't belong in soil,
so I recycled it."

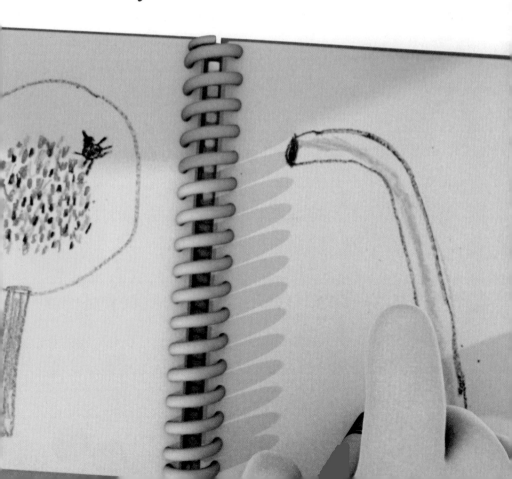

"I saw bits of leaves and twigs,"
said Sid.

"And a cool-looking worm.
I put him back in the dirt."

"Worms are good for the soil,"
said Teacher Susie.

"I'm proud of all of you.

You know a lot about keeping

the Earth healthy."

Next the kids had a birthday party
for the Earth.

"I'll be the Earth!" said Gerald.

"Make a birthday wish," said May.

"I wish to be clean," said Gerald.

"We can all help," said Sid.

"I can walk more places so we don't use the car so much," said Gabriela.

"And I can recycle," said May.

"We can do a lot to help the Earth."

When Sid got home,

he and Dad planted the baby tree.

"Trees make the Earth happy,"

said Sid.

"And healthy soil helps

baby trees grow into big trees."

"Caring for the Earth feels good.

Plus, it is fun to get dirty!"

LAUGHTERNOON

a good time for some earthy jokes

What did the worm's mom say when he came home late?
Where on Earth have you been?

What do trees drink?
Root beer.

What do you get when you wear a purple cowboy hat, pink pants, and orange shoes and then jump in a mud puddle?
You get . . . dirty!

What do you get when you take all the trees, and all the oceans, and all the animals, and all the soil?
The Earth! Happy Earth Day!